Summer Song

BY Kevin Henkes

ILLUSTRATED BY Laura Dronzek

GREENWILLOW BOOKS
An Imprint of HarperCollins*Publishers*

Summer Song

Manufactured in China. For information address
HarperCollins Children's Books, a division of HarperCollins Publishers,
195 Broadway, New York, NY 10007.
www.harpercollinschildrens.com

Acrylic paints were used to prepare the full-color art.
The text type is 32-point Bernhard Gothic SG Medium.

Library of Congress Cataloging-in-Publication Data

Names: Henkes, Kevin, author. | Dronzek, Laura, illustrator.
Title: Summer song / by Kevin Henkes ; illustrated by Laura Dronzek.
Description: First edition. | New York, NY : Greenwillow Books, an imprint of HarperCollinsPublishers, [2020] |
Summary: Illustrations and easy-to-read text introduce the colors, songs, and activities of summer.
Identifiers: LCCN 2018034450| ISBN 9780062866134 (trade ed.) | ISBN 9780062866141 (lib. bdg.)
Subjects: | CYAC: Summer—Fiction. | Seasons—Fiction.
Classification: LCC PZ7.H389 Ss 2020 | DDC [E]—dc23
LC record available at https://lccn.loc.gov/2018034450

20 21 22 23 24 SCP 10 9 8 7 6 5 4 3 2 1
First Edition

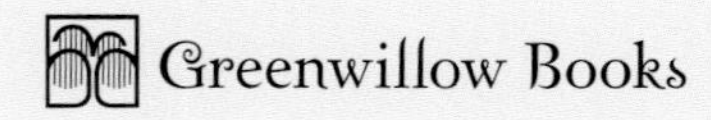

For Will and Clara

The Summer sun is a giant flower,
and the flowers are like little suns.
Little suns of all different colors.

But if I had to pick one color,
I'd say Summer is green.
Green on green on green.
Summer is a green song.

A song of leaves

and trees

and weeds

and grass,
lots of grass.

If there is tall grass in a field
and the wind blows,
it sounds like music.

So do the air conditioners

and the fans

and the sprinklers

and the lawn mowers.

Most of the time, birds are part of the song—
in the air, of the sky—

and sometimes rain and thunder are, too.

If you lie in the grass,
and you're quiet and patient and lucky,
you might hear a bug song—
whirring and buzzing and humming.

Are there bees?
Yes.

Grasshoppers?
Yes.

Crickets?
Yes.

Dragonflies?

Yes.

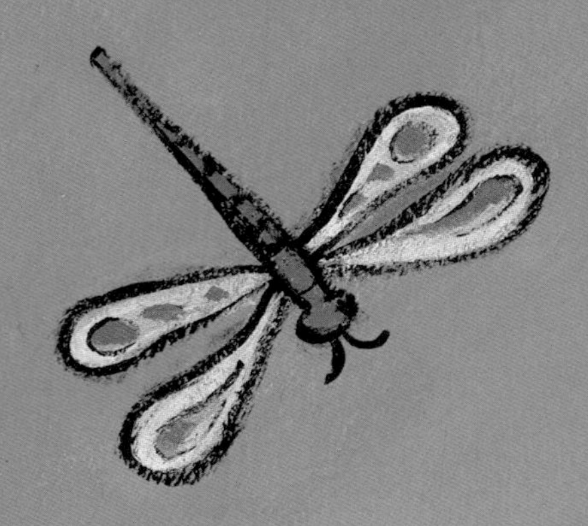

And silent butterflies, too.

And at night are there fireflies?
Sometimes.
There's one!
And another one!

And another one!

And another one!

They're singing to each other
without a sound.

When there is fog early in the morning,
Summer is a gray song.

When you go to the beach or a lake,
Summer is a blue song.
And when the sky is blue, too.

But the green song is still there.

If you slow down and think about it,
you can feel the Summer song.

It's warm

and then hot

and then hotter.

In the shade it can be cool,

or when you play with the hose.

But when the days become shorter
and the nights come earlier,
the song changes.

Summer gets bored
and wants to try something new,
something different.

The song is turning
turning
turning . . .

it's turning into Fall.